W9-BLP-724

3 5086 00076 3688

+
G116i

Ida Fanfanny

BY DICK GACKENBACH

HARPER & ROW, PUBLISHERS

NEW YORK, HAGERSTOWN, SAN FRANCISCO, LONDON

IDA FANFANNY
Copyright © 1978 by Dick Gackenbach
All rights reserved. No part of this book may be used or reproduced in any
manner whatsoever without written permission except in the case of brief
quotations embodied in critical articles and reviews. Printed in the United
States of America. For information address Harper & Row, Publishers, Inc.,
10 East 53rd Street, New York, N.Y. 10022. Published simultaneously in Canada
by Fitzhenry & Whiteside Limited, Toronto.
FIRST EDITION

Library of Congress Cataloging in Publication Data
Gackenbach, Dick
  Ida Fanfanny.

  SUMMARY: Ida lives in a land of no weather until
a salesman sells her four magical paintings.
  [1. Seasons—Fiction]   I. Title.
PZ7.G117Id   [E]   77-25656
ISBN 0-06-021953-X
ISBN 0-06-021954-8 lib. bdg.

For Christopher Reichenbach

Ida Fanfanny lived in a small wooden house in the middle of the Valley of Glebe. It was the only house in the whole valley. But Ida did not lack for good company. She shared her house with Gert, her goose, and Dan, her gander.

In all her life, Ida had never suffered through a day of bad weather in Glebe Valley. But then, she had never enjoyed a day of good weather either. There was no weather at all in Glebe. No seasons ever passed there. No sun or moon or clouds of any kind ever filled the sky above the rocks that covered Ida's land.

The towering mountains of Yurt, surrounding the rocky valley, rose so high that no sun or moon was ever able to rise above their peaks. And no matter how hard the weather clouds pushed and shoved against the mountains, they could never roll across the lofty summits.

No wonder then, when an occasional hardy peddler braved the terrifying mountain heights in search of business, his traditional greeting would baffle Ida Fanfanny.

"Nice weather we are having," he would say. Or, "We could use a little rain."

"The climb must have touched his head," Ida would whisper to Dan.

And the silly, useless things they had to sell would send Ida and the geese into peals of laughter. Galoshes, umbrellas and weather vanes! Hoes and rakes and fans!

"Fancy those, Gert," Ida would giggle.

She did buy an umbrella once. She thought it would make a perfect bed for Gert and Dan. And so it did.

Then one sunless, rainless, windless day, a very special peddler arrived at Ida's door. He was a dapper fellow, and Harvey Cellalotti was his name. He came on foot and pulled his heavy cart across the rocky surface of Glebe Valley.

"If you're selling nonsense, like galoshes or earmuffs, don't bother to unpack," Ida greeted him sourly.

"You will find none of that in my cart, Madam," replied Mr. Cellalotti, with some pride. "I carry an exclusive line of fine enchanted paintings. Paintings that hold the gift of magic for any lucky purchaser."

"Enchanted, you say? Magical, you say?" questioned Ida, with more than just a gleam of interest.

"Indeed so!" continued the peddler. "For they are painted with brushes made only from the hairs plucked from the tails of apes in the Fuudad Islands. And the colors are mixed only from feathers, freely given, by the mystic Moan Birds."

"Well," said Ida thoughtfully, "I could use a little magic in my life."

Gert and Dan heartily agreed.

When Ida saw the paintings, she was so impressed with their beauty, she decided to buy three of the finest ones Mr. Cellalotti had. The three were called *Spring*, *Summer*, and *Fall*. The one called *Fall* was especially colorful.

Mr. Cellalotti was so pleased with his large sale, he gave Ida an extra painting at no charge at all.

"It would be a shame to break up a set," he said. The free painting was called *Winter*.

"Now, the directions for the magic, should you care to use it, are printed clearly on the back of each painting," Mr. Cellalotti told Ida. "And if you are not fully satisfied, your money will be cheerfully refunded," he added. Then, with a lighter cart than before, he headed back across the rocks towards the mountains of Yurt.

Even before Mr. Cellalotti was out of sight, Ida hung the painting called *Spring* on her wall, but not before she read the directions very carefully.

To start *or* stop magic:

Squeeze eyes shut and see nothing.
Close ears and hear nothing.
Hold head upright and sing your
favorite song with gusto.

MAGIC ABSOLUTELY GUARANTEED

"Well," said Ida, to Gert and Dan, "I'll give it a try."

So, full of excitement, Ida began to follow the directions exactly. She squeezed her eyes shut as tight as she could, and covered her ears firmly with her hands. Then she sang out a rousing version of "Oh, Dem Golden Slippers." But nothing happened. She sang the song once more, but still nothing happened.

Gert pecked lightly on Ida's leg.

"What is it, Gert? What is it?" snapped Ida.

"Your favorite song," said Gert calmly, "is 'She'll Be Comin' Round the Mountain!' "

"Oh, and so it is, dear goose," cried Ida.

Her good humor restored, Ida sang out again, and with great feeling, "She'll be comin' round the mountain when she comes. She'll be comin' round the mountain when she comes."

It was no easy task for magic to move someone the size of Ida Fanfanny, but move her it did. By the time she reached the second chorus, "She'll be drivin' six white horses," Ida's feet began to leave the floor. Then, as though carried by some wind, Ida weaved and bobbed through the air like a mighty butterfly. And on the last chorus, "We'll be singin' Hallelujah when she comes," Ida drifted into the painting called *Spring* the way a thread fits into the eye of a needle.

When Ida opened her eyes, she saw a bright blue sky, filled with white billowing clouds.

"Dear me, what a sight," she gasped, for she had never seen a blue sky or clouds before.

When Ida uncovered her ears, she heard the sounds of singing birds. The earth smelled sweet and new, and was covered, not with rocks like Glebe Valley, but with buttercups and blue-eyed marys, violets and fiddle-head ferns as far as her eye could see.

"How much I have missed in the valley," sighed Ida.

Suddenly, a gentle spring rain began. Ida found joy in this too, for she had never been in the rain before. She lifted her head to the sky and began to dance, while the raindrops bounced off her big round nose.

"I will go back for Gert and Dan, and we will live here in Spring forever," Ida sang, for her heart was full of happiness.

But the spring rain went on and on. Soon the water seemed to be pouring from the sky.

"Does it never stop?" wondered Ida.

It rained so hard, the banks of the rippling brook overflowed and sent its water rushing headlong towards a wet and bewildered Ida.

To save herself from the flood, Ida quickly climbed the nearest tree.

"Nasty bit of business," she said, clinging to the limb of the sturdy oak.

When the flood was gone, Ida climbed down from the safety of the tree, only to discover her beautiful land of Spring had turned into a bog of gooey mud.

"I want no more of this," decided Ida.

She squeezed her eyes shut to all the sights of Spring, and covered her ears firmly to all its sounds.

"Oh, we'll all go out to meet her when she comes," she sang.

And so the same magic that had brought Ida into Spring carried her back home to the weatherless Valley of Glebe.

The wet and muddy traveler was given a warm greeting by Gert and Dan, although she had not been gone for a very long time.

"And what did you think of Spring?" they asked.

"You can't depend on it," Ida told the geese.

She removed *Spring* from the wall, and hung in its place the picture called *Summer.*

"Perhaps here I can find some magic that is not so fickle."

The directions for *Summer* were no different from those for *Spring*, except Ida was to hum her favorite song. Now, to sing with gusto is easy, but to hum with all your heart and soul is a very difficult thing to do. However, even with her eyes and ears closed, Ida was able to manage so lusty a hum of "She'll Be Comin' Round the Mountain," she was lifted away into *Summer* with no delay.

Summer was like a festival for Ida.

"The earth is like a big green pillow," she said, as she sat down on the soft grass. She lifted her head towards the warm golden sun and sniffed the summer breeze. For a long time she watched as the wind made the willow trees dance.

"Oh, how much I have missed living in a land with no sun or gentle breezes."

Happily, Ida munched on the fat blueberries that covered the bushes, and sucked on the tender grapes from the vines.

But all too soon, the Summer sun grew very hot, and the air became warm and sticky. The greenbottle flies buzzed everywhere. Crawling red ants and wandering stink bugs found their way up Ida's legs.

"Off, off," she demanded, but still they came.

Worst of all, the mosquitoes found Ida very tasty.

SWAT. "Got you," she cried, but Ida could not swat them all.

Then came the moths and the hornets, the gnats and caterpillars too, until Ida was fairly covered with bugs.

Ida was so busy fighting the bugs and trying to cool off, she hadn't noticed that the sky had darkened, nor had she heard the rumbling in the distance. Not until the wind blew hard and hail pounded down on the crown of her head did she notice the fierce black clouds above her. She looked up just in time to see the first shots of lightning streak from the sky and strike the earth with a shattering roar.

"It's the Devil's work," screamed the terrified Ida. She wanted to return home as fast as she could. Ida covered her ears and shut her eyes, but was too frightened to remember the tune she was supposed to hum. A fresh bolt of lightning split the sky and brought her memory back with a bang.

"She'll be comin' round the mountain when she comes," Ida hummed as snappily as she could. Soon she was safe back home in the Valley of Glebe.

"My," said Gert when she saw Ida, "you always return soaking wet."

"How was Summer?" asked Dan.

"Don't ask," replied Ida. But then, with her heart still pounding hard, she told the geese about her very first thunderstorm.

"For your sake, I don't think you should leave home again," advised Dan.

But Ida was still curious. She removed *Summer* from the wall and replaced it with *Fall*.

"It certainly looks calm enough," said Ida, as she studied the painting, "and, oh, so beautiful."

This time, Ida was instructed to whistle her favorite song to work the magic. Since Ida was a very good whistler, she had no trouble at all entering *Fall*.

Ida was quite amazed with the beauty she found in *Fall*, for she had never seen so many vivid colors in all her life. But she was also very cautious.

She took a long look about her.

"There don't seem to be many bugs here," she said. She scanned the sky.

"No signs of black clouds or driving rains that I can see."

Then she checked the wind. It was cool, but bracing.

"So far, so good," she said. Ida had never seen so much golden corn or so many shiny apples. And the leaves on the trees glowed with color.

"Nothing could happen to spoil this beauty," she decided.

But just when Ida relaxed and settled down, ready to enjoy it all, a north wind blew in. It shook the trees with such an enormous force that all the beautiful colors were torn from the trees and tossed to the ground like confetti.

Ida took one look at the once-splendid trees, now bare and gray, and burst into tears.

"Oh, shoo," said Ida.

Sad and angry, without wasting another minute there, Ida left Fall and whistled her way back to the Valley of Glebe.

Ida's tears were barely dry when she returned to Gert and Dan.

"Well, at least you're not all wet this time," said Gert.

"What was Fall like?" asked Dan.

"A will-o'-the-wisp, a house of cards," Ida answered sadly.

"Nothing ever lasts," sighed Dan. "Poor old thing," he said, as he put his beak on Ida's shoulder.

Now Ida had only one more picture left—*Winter*.

"No wonder it was free," she said as she looked at it. "There is nothing there."

Ida checked the instructions, which were clear and much the same as before. Only this time Ida was instructed to fiddle her way to *Winter*.

"Lucky you have a fiddle, and can fiddle well," said Gert.

"But how can I fiddle and hold my ears shut at the same time?" Ida wondered.

"Put cotton in your ears, silly," said Gert.

It sometimes bothered Ida that she had a goose smarter than she was.

"Thank you," muttered Ida, as she stuffed her ears with cotton and shut her eyes very tight. Then, with great skill and not one sour note, Ida fiddled her way into *Winter*.

Ida had entered *Winter* with little hope of finding much there, but what she found delighted her. The evergreen trees dripped with snow, like blobs of whipped cream. The icy frost had dressed the shrubs with delicate lace. Everything was silent and white and beautiful.

"Winter has a majesty all its own," remarked Ida. "It is more regal and grand than any other place I've been."

As Ida stared about her in wonder, the snowflakes began to fall. She caught the tiny crystals on her tongue, and it was not long before she discovered how to slide down slippery hills and glide across the frozen waters.

"I've never had so much fun," she laughed.

But Ida was not dressed for Winter, and soon she became very cold. Her toes grew numb and her ears began to hurt, her nose dripped and she began to sneeze and sniffle.

"Ach-choo," she sneezed. "I-I b-b-better g-g-go home," said Ida wisely, for she was nearly frozen to the bone. But her fiddle was nowhere in sight.

"W-w-where's my f-f-fiddle?" cried Ida. There was no way she could get home without it.

She searched everywhere. She looked beneath a log, behind some icy bushes, even below the frozen waters, but Ida could not find the fiddle anywhere.

Frightened and tired, and growing colder every minute, poor shivering Ida sat down on a clump of snow, hoping to find a way out of her dilemma. When she sat down there was a small crunch, and Ida found her fiddle under the fresh snow. Fortunately, very little damage was done and the fiddle was still very fiddlable.

"I-I'm so glad I d-d-don't have to s-s-sing," she said.

So with fingers stiff and numb, Ida fiddled away. "She'll be comin' round the mountain when she comes." Fiddling and floating across the snow, Ida drifted away from winter, back to the Valley of Glebe.

"You're wet again," screamed Gert when she saw Ida.

Dan began to rush around and made a good hot soup for his cold friend.

While Ida thawed out and sipped her soup, she wondered what she might do now with her magic paintings.

"Definitely demand your money back," insisted Dan.

Ida hung all four paintings on the wall, and as she looked them over, *Spring* did not seem so fickle, nor *Summer* quite so hot. *Fall* certainly had its beauty while it lasted, and *Winter*, if you dressed for it, might not be too cold.

"Each had its good points," said Ida with a sigh.

"Well, then," said Gert firmly, "enjoy them while the magic lasts, and when it fades, move on."

"You are a wonder, Gert," shouted Ida, "to have thought of that."

Ida Fanfanny, along with Gert and Dan, did just that, and the rest of their life was always full of magic.

And if some peddler was lucky enough to find them
back home in the Valley of Glebe, there was always
a great need for such things as
> fans and lightning rods,
> rakes and hoes,
> galoshes,
> umbrellas
> and, most of all,
> a weather vane.